MATT CHRISTOPHER®

#1
ONE SMOOTH MOVE

Text by **Stephanie Peters**
Illustrated by **Michael Koelsch**

LITTLE, BROWN AND COMPANY

New York ⌒ Boston

Little, Brown and Company

Time Warner Book Group
1271 Avenue of the Americas, New York, NY 10020
Visit our Web site at www.lb-kids.com

First Edition

The characters and events portrayed in this book are fictitious.
Any similarity to real persons, living or dead, is coincidental
and not intended by the author.

Matt Christopher® is a registered trademark
of Catherine M. Christopher.

Library of Congress Cataloging-in-Publication Data
Christopher, Matt.
One smooth move / Matt Christopher ; text by Stephanie Peters.
p.   cm. — (The extreme team ; #1)
Summary: When his family moves into his recently deceased
grandmother's house, ten-year-old Charlie meets a boy who also likes to
skateboard, but then finds that his own special skateboard is missing.
ISBN 0-316-73746-1 (hc) / ISBN 0-316-73749-6 (pb)
[1. Moving, Household — Fiction.   2. Skateboarding — Fiction.
3. Friendship — Fiction.]   I. Peters, Stephanie.   II. Title.
PZ7.C458On 2004   2003048829
[Fic] — dc21

HC: 10   9   8   7   6   5   4   3   2   1
PB: 10   9   8   7   6   5   4   3   2   1

WOR (hc)

COM-MO (pb)

Printed in the United States of America

CHAPTER ONE

Charlie Abbott put one foot on his skateboard and pushed off with the other. He gained some speed, then put both feet on and coasted. It was one smooth ride on a beautiful end-of-summer day. But Charlie wasn't enjoying it.

Another new neighborhood! he thought dismally.

Charlie was ten years old. He and his parents had moved seven times. He'd lived in seven new houses, been to seven new schools, gotten to know seven new neighborhoods. And seven times, he'd tried to fit in and make friends.

Now they'd moved for the eighth time. And did

he believe his mom when she said this was the last house he'd live in? No, he did not!

Immediately, he felt guilty. The new house was special to his mother. It had belonged to *her* mother, Charlie's grandmother. Grandma Beth had died a few months ago.

"I'm not selling it," his mother had said to his father. "It's the house I grew up in. I want Charlie to grow up in it, too." And just like that, they sold their old house, packed up their belongings, and moved — again.

Charlie zigzagged down the sidewalk. His mom was so sad when her mother died. Charlie was sad, too. He had always been able to tell Grandma Beth anything. Sometimes, she seemed to understand Charlie better than his parents did.

Take sports, for example. Charlie liked to play catch with his dad and shoot hoops with his mom. Whenever they moved, his parents encouraged him to join one of the teams. "It's a great way to make friends!" his dad would say.

CHAPTER TWO

Charlie coasted to a stop in front of his house. With a stomp of his foot, he popped his board up into his hands.

"Cool move."

Charlie swung around.

There stood a boy about his own age. He had one foot on a skateboard. A mop of black hair stuck out from under his helmet.

"You been surfing the pavement long?" the boy asked.

Charlie shrugged. "I've been skateboarding for about two years, I guess," he answered.

"So how come I've never seen you at the skate-park?"

Charlie's ears pricked up. "There's a skatepark around here?"

The boy didn't answer. He was too busy staring at Charlie's board. "Whoa. That board is awesome! Can I hold it?"

Charlie hesitated. After all, he didn't even know this kid's name.

But what's he gonna do, jump on and ride off? Charlie thought. He handed the board to the boy.

The boy spun the red wheels, then traced the red designs with his finger. He pointed to the "C.A."

"What's that stand for?" he asked.

"My name, Charlie Abbott."

"I'm X," the boy said. When Charlie looked confused, he laughed and added, "It's short for Xavier. Xavier McSweeney." He handed the board back to Charlie. "So, are you here to check out the new family? My mom sent me to get the four-one-one on them."

"The what?"

"The four-one-one," X repeated, eyebrows raised. "Don't you know what that means?"

Charlie shook his head.

"Four-one-one is the phone number you dial for information, right? So getting the four-one-one means getting information. Sheesh, I thought everyone knew *that*."

Charlie reddened.

"So, you know what I heard?" X said. "I heard the old lady who used to live there *died* in that house! When they carried her out, she looked like this." He crossed his eyes, stuck his tongue out of the side of his mouth, and turned his hands into claws. "Man," he said, going back to normal, "there's no way *I'd* live in a house where someone died. What if her ghost came through the bathroom door when you were, you know, doing your business?" He shuddered. "No way!"

Charlie frowned. He didn't like X calling Grandma Beth an "old lady" or making fun of her death. Besides,

he knew for a fact that Grandma Beth had died in a hospital. He decided to set X straight — to give him the 4-1-1.

"Listen —"

X interrupted, "So you wanna go rip it up over at the skatepark?" Without waiting for Charlie to answer, he kicked off on his skateboard.

Charlie was torn. He wanted to see the skatepark. Then again, he was still burning from X's little death performance.

But he didn't know she was your grandmother, he reminded himself. *And what else are you going to do now? Watch moving men unload furniture? Snoresville!*

He put his board to the pavement and shoved off.

CHAPTER THREE

Minutes later, Charlie stood open-mouthed at the skatepark gate. In front of him was a slice of extreme-sports heaven. The park was chock full of equipment. Ramps, pyramids, and boxes took up one part. In another were grinding rails of different heights. And in the center, not one but *two* half pipes, complete with decks. There was even an obstacle course.

"Are you going in or what?" X shoved past Charlie. Charlie was about to put his board down and follow him when a hand pulled him back.

"Hold on just one second."

The hand belonged to a teenage girl with a spiky

hairstyle and almond-shaped eyes. "You're new here, aren't you?"

"His name's Charlie and he's with me, Alison," X said.

Alison relaxed her grip and grinned. "Sorry to hear that, Charlie," she said. "Ever been to a skate-park before?"

"Yeah. My old town had one. But it wasn't anywhere near as good as this one."

Alison nodded. "Yeah, this is decent. Top of the line and brand new. We almost didn't get half this stuff, either."

Suddenly, her eyes narrowed. "'Scuse me." She stuck her fingers in her mouth and let out a piercing whistle. "Hey, you, on the half pipe!" she bellowed. Her voice was so loud Charlie couldn't believe it came out of her small body. "Wait your turn or you're out of here!"

The girl on the half pipe quickly sat down.

"So anyway," Alison resumed in a normal voice, "the community center gets permission to build the park, right? But there's not a whole lot of money for equipment. We're thinking, great, the park is going to be lame. Then, out of the blue, someone donates a whole big wad of cash to the project. So instead of a dinky little park we got this beauty." She gazed out at the park with pride.

"Who gave the money?" Charlie asked.

"The donor was anonymous." She gave a sly grin. "But I'm working on finding out. One of these days, I'll have the answer."

She turned to Charlie and gave him the once-over. "Okay, before I let you in, you've gotta pass my little test. Ready?"

Charlie nodded.

"First, board down to that fence and back."

Charlie shoved off, gained some speed, then zig-zagged to the fence. Without stopping, he swung around and boarded back to Alison.

"Not bad," she said. "Can you do an ollie?"

Charlie put his right foot near the tail of the board and his left near the center. Then he stomped his right

foot down hard. At the same time, he slid his left foot forward and jumped into the air. His board came up with him as if it was attached to his feet. He landed cleanly, both feet still on the board.

"You catch some good air, kid," Alison said. "Can you do street and vert skating?"

"I'm better at the rails than the ramps," Charlie admitted. "I can grind and slide, but I'm still working on doing spins and grabs off the ramps."

"Okay, you're in," Alison said. She held up a warning finger. "But I'll be keeping my eye on you. If I see you trying something you can't handle, I'll throw you out faster than you can say Tony Hawk. Got it?"

"Got it!"

CHAPTER FOUR

Charlie headed straight for his favorite piece of equipment, the rails. Remembering Alison's warning, he decided to do his first grind on a low one.

He pushed off and skated toward the rail. When he was close enough, he popped an ollie. He and his skateboard jumped into the air. Both the skateboard's trucks landed cleanly on the higher end of the rail. Holding his arms out for balance, he slid from one end of the rail to the other. Then the rail ended, and Charlie and the board dropped safely to the ground.

"Nice fifty-fifty grind!" Charlie looked up to see X grinning at him. "Wanna trade boards for a while?"

Charlie eyed X's board. Compared to his own

gleaming black-and-red one, X's looked shabby. The grip tape on top was worn and there was a small nick on the nose.

"It's got a couple of battle wounds," X admitted, "but it still works. C'mon, let's trade!"

"Okay," Charlie said reluctantly. He took the board from X and flipped it over to examine it more closely. The blue-and-orange paint on the bottom deck was scratched in places. He put it on the ground and took a few practice rides. His own board felt smoother.

Meanwhile, X was testing Charlie's board. "This is so totally rad," he said. "Can I try jumping over a rail with it?" X looked so hopeful, Charlie didn't have the heart to say no.

X chose a rail of medium height. He backed up until he was the right distance away. Then he rode at the rail. When he was close enough, he popped an ollie, sailed high over the rail, and landed hard with both feet still on the board. He let out a *whoop* and then called out, "Your turn!"

Charlie copied X's move. He didn't catch as much

air as X had, but he still cleared the rail with inches to spare.

They took turns jumping, then switched to grinds. X wasn't quite as good at these. He'd land on the rail okay, but he would wobble off halfway down. Each time his board clattered to the ground, Charlie hoped it wasn't getting nicked.

Finally, after an hour, the boys traded boards back. "I gotta get this thing in shape," X said, taking his board from Charlie. "Yours is awesome. Totally awesome."

"Thanks," said Charlie. Suddenly, his cell phone chirped. It was his mother calling, telling him to come home. "I gotta go."

"Yeah, me too," said X. "So, see you here tomorrow?"

Charlie knew his mother probably had "new house" stuff for him to do the next day, so he answered, "Yeah, maybe, maybe not."

X looked at him funny, then kicked off and

coasted to the park entrance. He and Charlie parted at the gate.

When Charlie got home, he stowed his skateboard in the garage. "Well, Charlie, you disappeared today!" his mother said when he came into the kitchen.

Charlie told her about the skatepark and about meeting X.

"Xavier McSweeney?" she asked. "His mother stopped by today with this pie. She told me about X. He's your age. Maybe he'll be in your class. Which reminds me, we're visiting your new school tomorrow morning."

Charlie sighed. He'd hoped to go to the skatepark in the morning. Now it would have to wait.

After dinner, his father asked him to help flatten and carry empty packing boxes to the garage. They worked for half an hour and built up a tall stack in one corner of the garage. When Charlie tried to toss his last boxes on top of the stack, the stack toppled over. Boxes landed everywhere.

"I'll take care of this mess," his father said kindly. "You look done in. Go on inside and relax."

Charlie yawned. "I guess I am a little tired." He dragged up to his bedroom, changed into his pajamas, and crawled into his bed. He read two pages in his book, then fell fast asleep.

CHAPTER FIVE

The next morning, Charlie put on a T-shirt and shorts. He wanted to take a quick ride down to the skatepark to see what time it opened. Maybe, if his appointment at school went fast enough, he'd be able to get in some boarding before lunch.

But when he looked for his skateboard in the garage, he couldn't find it. He searched high and low. It was nowhere to be found. Puzzled, Charlie returned to the kitchen to ask his mother if she or his dad had moved it. He didn't get a chance.

"We're due at the school in ten minutes!" his mother said. "Hurry and get changed."

Charlie reappeared a minute later wearing his usual "school enrollment" outfit: a navy blue shirt with a collar tucked into khaki pants. His dark hair was neatly combed. On his feet were brown loafers instead of sneakers.

"Oh, don't you look nice!" his mother exclaimed. Charlie thought he looked like a dork, but he knew better than to say so.

The rest of the morning was spent answering questions and filling out papers. Charlie saw his homeroom and met his new teacher, Mrs. Palmer. She and his mother got into a discussion. Charlie sat down and waited for them to finish.

"Hi there!"

A girl with wavy brown-black hair and skin the color of peanuts plopped down next to him. "Are you new?" she asked.

Charlie nodded. "You, too?"

"Naw, the school lost my paperwork, so we had to come in to do it again." She stuck out her hand. "My name's Bizz. That's short for Belicia."

Does everyone in this town have a nickname? Charlie wondered.

"Only my *abuela* calls me that," Bizz added. She narrowed her eyes at him. "You know what *abuela* means, right?"

He nodded. "It's Spanish for grandmother." Bizz grinned. Apparently, Charlie had passed some test of hers.

Charlie's mom beckoned him. "See you later, uh, Bizz," he said, standing up. She waved.

As they left the building, his mother said, "There's a restaurant downtown your grandmother used to like. Let's eat there, okay?" Charlie didn't argue.

In the restaurant, they sat near a big picture window. "I better make sure I have enough cash to pay for this," his mother said. She took out her wallet and opened it. Something fluttered out. She picked it up — and gasped.

Charlie looked up to see what was wrong. His mom was gripping a picture of Grandma Beth.

Her eyes filled with tears as she looked at the

photo. "I — I forgot I still had this in my wallet," she said. "Excuse me a sec, honey." She stood up and disappeared into the ladies' room.

Charlie sat frowning at his placemat, trying to think of a way to cheer up his mother when she returned. A movement outside the window caught his attention. Still frowning, he turned to see what it was.

X was walking by. Under his arm was a skateboard. But it wasn't the same beat-up skateboard he'd ridden the day before. This skateboard was black with red designs!

Charlie and X stared at each other. Then X blinked, turned away, and hurried quickly down the sidewalk. In a flash, he had disappeared around a corner.

Charlie couldn't believe it. *X had stolen his skateboard!*

CHAPTER SIX

Neither Charlie nor his mother ate much lunch. The car ride back to the house was silent, each of them lost in their own thoughts.

X stole my skateboard! The same sentence spun through Charlie's mind over and over.

Then Charlie shook himself. *Before I call him a thief, I better be sure.*

So he asked his mom if she had moved his skateboard. She hadn't. Neither had his dad. Charlie checked the garage again. He saw garbage cans, lawn equipment, and the stack of flattened boxes. No skateboard.

Charlie returned to the house and climbed the

stairs to his bedroom. He pulled out a box from his closet. Inside were his inline skates. Charlie sat holding the skates in his lap thinking, *I can blade to the park. See if X is there.* Exactly what he'd do if he found X with his board, he didn't know.

He carried the skates outside and snapped them on. He tugged his helmet into place and took off, skating slowly toward the park. He was halfway there when he heard someone call his name. He turned and saw Bizz skating toward him. Another girl — possibly the most beautiful girl Charlie had ever seen — was skating with her.

"Hey, Charlie!" Bizz said. "Are you heading to the skatepark?"

Charlie nodded. He tried not to stare at Bizz's friend.

"Savannah and I are going there too," Bizz said. "C'mon, let's race!" She took off, her feet a blur of movement. Savannah smiled at Charlie and hurried after Bizz.

Charlie scrambled to catch up. Savannah wasn't

very fast, but Bizz was a blur of motion. *Man,* he thought, *that girl can skate!*

Alison was at the park entrance again.

"So, the new kid can inline too, I see!" She waved the threesome through.

"Um, Alison? Have you seen X here?" Charlie asked after he'd caught his breath.

Bizz gave a little shout. "You know X? How crazy! We're meeting him and some other guys here!"

"He's over at the rails," Alison said. "He couldn't wait to get to them today."

Sure enough, when Charlie looked, X was flying over a high rail. Bizz and Savannah hurried to join him. Two other boys were there, too. Charlie hung back, watching. But his eyes weren't on any of the kids. They were on the board X was riding. As X popped an ollie, Charlie saw a flash of black and red. His heart sank.

He did *steal it,* he thought miserably. Until that moment, he hadn't wanted to believe it was true.

Further proof came seconds later. Bizz was talking with X. She pointed in Charlie's direction, and X looked over. As soon as Charlie made eye contact with him, X quickly rode away, leaving through the park's back entrance.

Bizz skated back to Charlie. She looked puzzled.

"That's weird. He just took off," she said. "I don't get it."

"Well, I do," Charlie burst out. "He stole my board — and he knows I saw him with it!"

CHAPTER SEVEN

Bizz gaped at him. She seemed incapable of speaking. Alison, on the other hand, spoke right up.

"Those are pretty strong words," she said, frowning. "What proof do you have?"

Before Charlie could reply, Bizz found her voice. "I don't care what proof he *thinks* he has," she thundered. "If he thinks X stole his board, he's *crazy!* X is one of the nicest, friendliest, most honest boys I know! He would *never* take something that didn't belong to him!"

Her fury was so intense that Charlie took a step backward before speaking.

"Look, all I know is, yesterday, X couldn't get

enough of my board. My *black-and-red* board," he added pointedly. "Yesterday, X's board was blue and orange. Today, I can't find my board — and X shows up riding a black-and-red one!"

"It's true, Bizz," Alison said reluctantly. "X was riding a different board this morning."

"That doesn't mean anything," Bizz said. Her lips were tight with anger.

"Oh, yeah?" Charlie replied. "If he didn't steal it, how come he took off the minute he saw me?"

"That does seem a little weird," Alison admitted.

Bizz adjusted her helmet. "Still doesn't mean any-thing," she muttered. With one last sour look at Char-lie, she spun and skated quickly back to her friends. When she reached them, she started talking and wav-ing her arms around wildly. At one point, all four looked over at him.

Charlie hadn't thought he could feel any worse. But that look made his toes curl inside his skates. He turned to leave.

"You know, there is one way you can find out

for sure if X took your board," Alison said thought-fully.

"How?" Charlie asked.

Alison looked him straight in the eye. "Ask him."

Charlie thought about Alison's suggestion the whole way home. Could he just flat out ask X if he'd taken his board?

He shook his head. No, he couldn't. What if he was wrong? He'd already made an enemy out of Bizz. Her friends, too, probably. Asking X about his board would just make X hate him too. There had to be another way. But what?

"Everything okay, Charlie?" his father asked after dinner. "Your lips have been zipped all night. Here, open 'em up and have some of this pie Mrs. Mc-Sweeney made."

Charlie looked away. Even though the pie smelled delicious, his stomach churned. There was no way he could eat even a bite of pie made by X's mother.

"That reminds me," Charlie's mom said. "I should get that pie plate back to Mrs. McSweeney. Charlie,

could you take it to her? They live just a few blocks away."

Going to X's house was the *last* thing Charlie wanted to do. But he couldn't think of a way out of it. So ten minutes later, he was ringing the McSweeneys' doorbell.

There was the sound of a dog barking and a chorus of voices. X's voice called out above the others. "I'll get it!"

Charlie's heart knocked inside his chest. He wanted to put the pie plate down and run away. He didn't have the chance. The door opened — and the two boys were standing face to face.

CHAPTER EIGHT

Charlie spoke first. "Here," he said, thrusting the pie plate at X. "My mom says thanks for the pie."

"Okay," X mumbled. He didn't look directly at Charlie, but he didn't close the door, either.

Suddenly, Charlie had an inspiration. Instead of accusing X of stealing his skateboard, he'd give X the chance to confess — or to return the board, no questions asked.

"So, you wanna meet at the skatepark tomorrow morning, do some more boarding?" Charlie asked.

X looked up, his face full of surprise. Then he broke out in a huge grin. "Sure, that'd be cool!" he said.

"The only thing is, I'll have to share your board with you," Charlie continued. "Mine's missing." He watched X's face very carefully for any sign of guilt. But X's expression didn't change.

Charlie felt a bubble of hope rise in his chest. *Maybe I am wrong!* he thought. Then X said something that popped the bubble.

"No prob. My board is your board." X started to shut the door. "Come around nine-thirty. That's when the kids I hang with show up."

Charlie walked home, more confused than ever. X hadn't seemed like he was hiding anything. In fact, he'd seemed relieved, even eager to go boarding with Charlie! Yet, what did he mean by "my board is your board"? Was that a confession? Or did it just mean that X didn't mind sharing his board?

"Oh, brother." Charlie groaned to himself. "My brain hurts."

His brain was still hurting the next morning. He snapped on his inline skates and made his way to the park. He was the first one there when Alison unlocked the gate at 9:30. He wasn't alone for long.

Next to arrive was Bizz. She frowned at Charlie and headed straight to the half pipe without saying a word. Charlie sighed and skated to the rails. He planned to practice jumping over them until X showed up.

Half an hour later, he was still practicing. Many more kids had come to the park, including some of the kids he'd seen with Bizz and X the day before. But there was no sign of X.

Should I try calling him? he wondered. He pulled out his cell phone, then realized he didn't know X's number. Besides, the phone was for emergencies only. He tucked the phone back into his pocket.

X still hadn't shown up by 10:20. Charlie had been skating alone for almost an hour. He was tired of jumping — and fed up with waiting.

"That's it. I'm outta here," he said to the empty air.

X must be some kind of actor. He sure had me fooled, he thought. *I really believed he wanted to meet me here today. That he wanted to be friends.*

Head down, Charlie skated toward the gate. His mood was as sour as a lemon. He didn't see X until he slammed right into him.

"You're still here!" X exclaimed.

"Surprised to see me?" Charlie sneered. "Well, take a good look, because the next thing you'll see is my back!" He shoved X aside and skated as fast as he could away from the skatepark.

CHAPTER NINE

Charlie didn't slow down until he got to his house. His breathing was ragged and his heart was hammering. Without bothering to take off his skates, he clumped across the lawn to a tree. He sat down heavily, drew his knees up, and rested his head on his arms.

I won't cry! I won't cry! he thought fiercely. But still his eyes welled up with tears.

Suddenly, he heard a shout.

"There he is! Under that tree!" Charlie didn't recognize the voice. He raised his head and looked around.

A young boy with dark skin and a flattop haircut

was pointing at him. A moment later, X joined him, followed closely by Bizz, Savannah, and another boy. All started toward him.

Charlie braced himself. Much as he wanted to run away, he couldn't get up easily because he still had his skates on. The last thing he wanted to do was fall on his face in front of them!

X was the first one to speak.

"Charlie, I think there's been a massive mix-up. Look." He thrust his skateboard into Charlie's hands. Charlie had no choice but to take it. He was certain he was holding his missing skateboard.

Then he looked at it more closely. True, this skateboard was shiny black with red designs, just like his. *But it wasn't his skateboard.* The designs were completely different. And this skateboard had a nick in the nose.

He stared up at X, speechless.

"I didn't steal your board, Charlie," X said quietly. "Your board looked so cool, I tried fixing up mine to look like it. But I didn't steal it."

Charlie wished the ground would swallow him up. He wanted to apologize to X, but all he could say was, "Oh."

Then something occurred to him. "Why did you take off when you saw me at the park the other day?"

Now it was X's turn to look uncomfortable. "Um, I, uh," he stammered.

"Oh, for Pete's sake, spit it out!" Bizz cried.

X nodded. "I felt bad for what I said about your grandmother. You know, making out like I was her dead body and all. I was trying to be funny." He kicked at the grass. "I didn't know she was your grandmother. My mom told me later that night, after she met your mom. So, um, sorry about that." Bizz nudged him. "Oh, yeah. Sorry about being so late this morning, too. I overslept."

Charlie thought about how X had changed his board to look like his. He thought about how much more fun he'd had jumping the rails with X than boarding by himself. He thought about how much he wanted to change Bizz's angry look to a friendly one. At last, he unsnapped his skates and stood up.

"And I'm sorry I thought you stole my board. So let's forget both things ever happened. Now," he added, "there are two last mysteries that need to be cleared up."

"What?" X asked.

"Number one, where is my skateboard? And number two," Charlie said, jerking a thumb at the two other boys, "who are these guys and do they have crazy nicknames too?"

CHAPTER TEN

The two other boys were introduced as Mark Goldstein and Jonas Malloy. "But you can call me Jonas," the kid with the flattop joked. "My bud X here tells me you can surf the pavement with the best of them. That grinding the rails is as easy for you as blowing a nostril slug into a tissue."

"Blowing a *what*?"

"Nostril slug." Bizz rolled her eyes. "That's Jonas's term for 'booger.' He likes to make up things like that. He thinks he's being creative."

"I *am* being creative!" Jonas shouted.

"Gross is more like it," Savannah murmured.

Laughing, X held up a hand. "Listen, it's time to take off our helmets and put on our detective hats," he said. He turned to Charlie. "Where's the last place you saw your board?"

"I put it in the garage the night we boarded together. In the morning it was gone."

"To the garage then, men!"

Bizz cleared her throat and Savannah raised an eyebrow.

"And women too, of course," X added hurriedly.

One by one they filed through the side door into the garage. Charlie flicked the light on. A quick look revealed the same stuff he'd seen the morning before: garbage cans, boxes, and lawn equipment. No skateboard.

Charlie sighed and reached over to flick the light off again. His hand accidentally hit the button for the garage door opener instead. The sudden sound and movement of the door opening startled Jonas. He jumped backward and bumped into the stack of moving boxes.

"Look out!" Charlie shouted. The whole stack came tumbling down, burying Jonas underneath.

Charlie and the others quickly pushed the boxes aside. Jonas stood up, rubbing his head. "Man, what are those things made of? Bricks?"

"Don't be such a baby," Bizz scoffed. "It's just cardboard."

"Yeah, well, something hard hit me, and it wasn't 'just cardboard'!"

"Wait a minute." X waded into the sea of boxes and started to feel around. Suddenly, he broke into a huge smile. From beneath the cardboard, he withdrew Charlie's skateboard!

"I don't believe it!" Charlie grabbed the board and hugged it to his chest. "How did it get stuck in there?"

"I think I can answer that question." The children turned to see Charlie's father enter the garage.

"Remember when all the boxes fell over the other night?" he asked. "When I cleaned them up, I just sort of shoved them into a stack. I guess I shoved your

skateboard in with them. Er, sorry. Hope it didn't cause any problems."

Charlie and X looked at each other and started laughing. The other kids joined in.

"No, Dad, no problem at all!" Still laughing, Charlie grabbed his board and yelled, "Last one to the skatepark is a nostril slug!"

Learn the Move! The Ollie

Do you already know how to ride a skateboard? If so, you may be ready to learn the first basic trick of skateboarding: the ollie. When you do an ollie, your board pops up underneath you. All four wheels clear the pavement as you and your board catch air. This jump is the basis for most skateboarding tricks. Before you can learn any other trick, you should master the ollie.

The best way to learn to do an ollie is to have someone who already knows how to do it show you. Otherwise, you can follow the steps on the next page. With practice and patience, you should get the hang of it!*

* *Remember, always wear your helmet and safety gear whenever skateboarding!*

Step one: Stand on your board and jump, landing with both feet back on the board. Be careful the skateboard doesn't shoot out from under you. This first step seems simple, but it requires balance and concentration. Once you feel comfortable with these jumps, move on to the next step.

Step two: Put your right foot on the tail, or back end, of the board. Put your left foot near the center but closer to the tail than the nose, or front end, of the board. You're now in ollie position.

Step three: To do the ollie, you have to do three things at the same time. 1) Stamp down on the tail with your right foot; 2) Slide your left foot forward toward the nose; and 3) Jump into the air. If you can do all three simultaneously — and land safely with both feet on the board — you can do an ollie!

THE EXTREME TEAM